JONES & PARKER CASE FILES

FOCUS ON THE FAMILY PRESENTS

Adventures in
ODYSSEY®

16 Mysteries to Solve Yourself

JONES & PARKER CASE FILES

Bob Hoose and Christopher P. N. Maselli

Tyndale House Publishers, Inc.
Carol Stream, Illinois

Jones and Parker Case Files: Sixteen Mysteries to Solve Yourself
© 2015 Focus on the Family

A Focus on the Family book published by Tyndale House Publishers, Inc., Carol Stream, Illinois 60188

Adventures in Odyssey and Focus on the Family and its accompanying logo and design are federally registered trademarks of Focus on the Family, 8605 Explorer Drive, Colorado Springs, CO 80920.

TYNDALE and Tyndale's quill logo are registered trademarks of Tyndale House Publishers, Inc.

Editor: Jesse Florea
Design by Beth Sparkman
Cover and interior illustrations by Gary Locke

These stories were previously published in *Adventures in Odyssey Clubhouse* magazine, formerly named *Focus on the Family Clubhouse*.

ISBN 978-1-58997-806-5

For manufacturing information regarding this product, please call 1-800-323-9400.

Printed in the United States of America
21
7   6   5   4

CONTENTS

Case File #2010-01

CASE OF THE SEALED SAFE

by Christopher P. N. Maselli

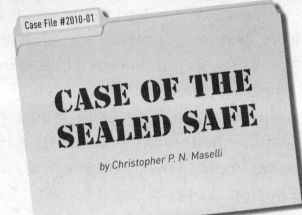

IN THE DETECTIVE AGENCY BUSINESS, cases can show up in the most unlikely places. Take last Monday, for example. My protégé, Matthew Parker, and I were waiting to get flu shots in the office of Dr. Lilly Graham, a new doctor in Odyssey. We went early so we wouldn't miss too many classes at school.

I have to admit, doctors' offices make me nervous—something about the smell of rubbing alcohol and disinfectant. This office was especially creepy because no other patients had arrived.

Come to think of it, the receptionist hadn't even arrived.

Suddenly from the back room, I heard a loud splat and a shriek of "Oh no!"

Just as suddenly, my detective instincts kicked in. "Hurry, Matthew. Someone's in trouble!"

I followed the sound down a hall to a quaint office. Freshly opened packing boxes and papers littered the floor. A small woman, who appeared older than my mother but younger than my grand-mother, was looking over a puddle of coffee on her desk. The tipped-over cup told me what I needed to know. The stethoscope around the woman's neck told me the rest.

Dr. Graham had spilled her coffee.

"Are you all right?" I asked.

"I'm just fine. Thanks for asking," the woman answered as she mopped up coffee with a paper towel.

"I'm Emily Jones, and this is Matthew Parker," I said.

"Jones and Parker?" she said. "As in the Jones and Parker Detective Agency?"

"You've heard of us?" Matthew said, wide-eyed.

"A patient told me about you yesterday," Dr.

Graham said. "You solved the mystery of his missing bow tie."

"Ah!" I said, remembering the case. "Alan Jakes and the Case of the Missing Neck Adornment."

Dr. Graham smiled. "It's good you're here this morning, because I now have a mystery to solve."

My ears perked up.

"A mystery?" Matthew asked. "Here? Now?"

Dr. Graham nodded. "That's right. I can't open the safe. I was about to call a locksmith, but since you're here—"

"My sidekick and I would love to help!" I said.

"I'm her *partner*," Matthew said.

"Sidekick," I whispered to Dr. Graham.

"I'm right *here*," Matthew said. "I can hear you."

Dr. Graham looked amused. "This is a first for me. I've never worked with such a *young* detective agency before."

"You can count on us!" I said, grabbing my detective notebook from my pocket. "Start from the top and leave nothing out."

Dr. Graham reached down and opened a large cabinet door. Inside was a black safe with a gold dial on the front. "This is the problem."

"It's a *safe*!" Matthew said.

I smiled. "He's keen at observation."

Matthew rolled his eyes.

"So what's the problem with it?" I asked.

"Well, as you may know," Dr. Graham said, "the previous doctor retired and handed his practice over to me. I was trying to get things organized when I found a note from Dr. Swink that said he put some patient files in the safe. But I don't have the combination."

"Did he forget to leave it for you?" I asked.

"No, Dr. Swink is one of the most meticulous people I've ever met. He left the combination in a note taped to the front of the safe. I had just pulled it off when my coffee spilled on it."

With two fingers she held up a small piece of notebook paper drenched in brown liquid. Only the top and bottom of the note were readable. The note was written in blue ink with a ballpoint pen, and the handwriting was neat.

I read:

I looked at the paper for a few moments, trying to decipher what I could.

"Why not just contact Dr. Swink?" Matthew asked.

"He's vacationing where there's no phone or email service on a remote island in the Caribbean," she replied.

"I could fly down and talk to him," I offered.

"I need those records *today*," Dr. Graham said, smiling at me.

A chime rang in the lobby, and Dr. Graham jumped up. "That must be my receptionist. I'll be right back."

"We'll keep sleuthing," I said.

"This is a tough one," Matthew said.

I knelt down and skimmed my finger along

the bottom of the safe. I grabbed the handle and pulled. It clicked but didn't open. I spun the dial and tried again. Nothing happened.

I turned my attention to the soaked note and noticed that the paper was the same color and size as a nearby notepad.

"May I borrow your pencil?" I asked Matthew.

He pulled it out from behind his ear. "What are you up to?" he asked.

"This is an old trick used by private eyes." I pressed the edge of the pencil against the top sheet of the notepad and lightly rubbed the gray lead back and forth.

"I get it!" Matthew said. "If Dr. Swink wrote a note on the top page of the pad, the pressure of the pen would make an impression on the page underneath."

"That's right." I held up the paper. We could see the impression of Dr. Swink's neat handwriting.

"Brilliant!" Matthew said.

"Mere detective work," I said, then frowned. "But this isn't the note he wrote to Dr. Graham."

"It looks like some kind of checklist," Matthew observed.

"He made a checklist on his last day in the office," I said.

Matthew shook his head. "He was really detailed. Look, he even scheduled time to 'remember.'"

"Interesting," I said. "Who schedules time to remember?"

Matthew laughed and pointed to the third check. "He left a *cod* on the safe. I bet that fish started to smell!"

I wasn't amused. "No, the *e* just didn't show through. It says he left the *code* on the safe."

Matthew pointed to numbers at the top. "Is that the code?"

"I assume that's the date he wrote the note," I said.

Matthew and I peered at the safe once more. It stared back at us defiantly.

Dr. Graham came back in the room. "Well? Have you figured out how to open the safe?"

I nodded. "I think so."

Matthew's eyebrows shot up. "What?!"

"The answer has been right in front of us this entire time," I stated.

"I can't wait to hear it!" Dr. Graham said.

I told them my solution. And I was *right*.

❆ ❆ ❆

Do *you* know how Emily opened the safe?

What are the clues?

Turn to the "Case Solved!" section on page 100 to find out.

Case File #2010-06

MYSTERY OF THE VANISHING PAINT

by Christopher P. N. Maselli

"THERE'S MR. WHITTAKER!" my sidekick, Matthew Parker, shouted as he ran into the Hardware Emporium. I followed reluctantly, because we were in the middle of brainstorming mottos for our detective agency. I didn't want to stop.

The best we'd come up with so far was "Jones and Parker: We hit the marker." We hadn't been brainstorming long.

"That's the strangest thing," Mr. Whittaker was saying to Mr. Watson, the owner of the hardware store. Then he turned to Matthew. "Well, hello there! What brings you by?"

Matthew smiled and shrugged. "Emily and I were just brainstorming mottos for the detective agency. What do you think of this? 'Jones and Parker: Mysteries are history.'"

Mr. Whittaker's white eyebrows rose. "Not bad. I'm actually in the middle of a mystery myself. Maybe your inventive minds could help."

My heart skipped a beat. I stepped forward. "The Jones and Parker Detective Agency can help. No mystery is too small, and neither are we!"

Matthew leaned toward Mr. Whittaker and whispered, "The motto's still being worked on."

Whit chuckled. "So I see."

"It's really not much of a mystery," Mr. Watson piped up. "Mr. Whittaker can't find the paint he's looking for."

"But I saw it in your shop not 30 minutes ago!" Whit said. "It was right over there." He pointed toward the front window. "As I was walking by outside, I saw it clear as day: a whole stack of gallon-size paint canisters. The entire bottom row was bright green—exactly the color I need for my latest invention."

Matthew's eyes lit up. "What're you working on?"

"Still top secret." Mr. Whittaker winked.

"I don't know what to tell you," Mr. Watson said. "We haven't sold any paint today. If we had green paint there, it would still be there."

Mr. Whittaker explained that he had seen the paint through the window, but stopped to talk to local handyman Red Hollard before buying it. Mr. Whittaker fig-ured it would still be there when he returned since there was a large stack.

I inspected the stack of paint cans still displayed by the window. Each canister was similar except for a label on the front, indicating the color. They were stacked in rows of blue, orange, purple, and yellow.

"Mr. Watson, could one of your employees have moved some of the cans?" I asked.

"Afraid not. I'm the only one here this morn-ing," Mr. Watson said. "And what you see is all we've got. But I'll give you a good deal on another color, Whit."

Whit shook his head. "No, thank you. I really needed that green."

I wanted to believe Whit, but the evidence was stacked against him. (Yes, that pun was intended. Puns are staples in detective reports. And yes, that pun was intended, too.)

Matthew crawled around on his knees, staring at the floor between the window and the first row of blue paint. He picked at the carpet fibers.

"What are you looking for, Matthew?" I asked.

"Evidence," he said simply.

"Matthew likes to get dirty," I said. "That's what makes us such good partners."

Matthew pumped his arm in victory. "She called me her partner!"

I couldn't believe I had let that slip. I wouldn't want my sidekick to get a big head.

"And, *partner*," Matthew said, "I'm observing that there's enough room between the window and the blue paint cans to fit a row of green paint . . . but there's no indentation in the carpet." He rubbed the window and left streaks in the yellowy dust that covered the bottom of it. "Are you

sure of what you saw, Mr. Whittaker? The window's pretty dirty."

Mr. Whittaker chuckled and removed his round glasses. "Maybe my glasses are failing. I guess that's a good example of how our eyes can fool us. But I was sure of what I saw. There was a row of green cans. Right there. Oh well, I'll get the paint somewhere else."

Mr. Whittaker turned to leave. I looked back at the stacks of paint cans. "Wait, Mr. Whittaker! I know what happened. You did see green paint!"

* * *

How can Emily be certain?

What are the clues?

Turn to the "Case Solved!" section on page 101 to find out.

Case File #2010-11

THANKSGIVING RUSH

by Christopher P. N. Maselli

B EING A PRIVATE investigator means being on your game at all times. Unfortunately, that can mean 5:00 a.m. on the day after Thanksgiving.

My lug of a brother, Barrett, somehow talked me into getting up early so we could stand in line outside Greenblatt's Department Store. He promised me I could find some *great* early-bird Christmas gifts for Mom and Dad . . . but I knew why he *really* wanted to go. He'd been saving for the *Verminoids Special Edition* video game.

"They're only releasing 10 games per store!" he exclaimed. "It has 20 new levels. *Twenty!*"

Mom and Dad wouldn't let him go alone, so I reluctantly volunteered on the condition that we would find Mom's and Dad's gifts first. I tried to get my sidekick, Matthew Parker, to join us, but he just laughed and said he'd think of me as he counted Zs.

At exactly 5 o'clock, the clerk unlocked the door. The line of cold shoppers cheered.

"Get ready to run!" Barrett shouted.

Suddenly the doors flew open and the crowd stampeded in. We squeezed our way in and headed to the music aisle. I spotted the CD Mom wanted and grabbed one from the stack on the endcap.

"Got it!" I shouted triumphantly.

"We gotta go! We gotta go!" Barrett shouted, pulling a wrinkled newspaper ad out of his pocket. He unfolded it quickly, slightly tearing the thin paper. "Dad would like this book."

I took the ad from him and scanned the store.

"Over there!" I pointed to a large sign that read "BOOKS."

We dashed through the men's clothing department and got to the book just before a crowd of others.

"Got it!" Barrett handed the book to me. "Now to get my video game! This way."

As we arrived in the electronics department, a Greenblatt's employee grabbed the sign above the Verminoids games. It read *"VERMINOIDS SPECIAL EDITION—ONLY 10 GAMES LEFT!"*

With the bold stroke of his black permanent marker, the employee crossed out the number 10.

Barrett's face turned white.

"Oh no," he said. "We're too late. They're all out."

My stomach twisted. I felt horrible.

"I'm so sorry, Barrett. I know you worked hard to save for your game."

"That's all right," he said, a disappointed look on his face. "At least we got Mom's and Dad's gifts. I'm thankful for that."

"Right. And you have a sister who's willing to

stand out in the freezing cold with you when she would have rather stayed in bed."

"Yeah, and that, too." He smiled.

As we turned to leave, the same employee drew the number "1" on the sign.

Barrett's eyes widened.

"There's *one left*!" Barrett shouted.

Suddenly, my lug of a brother turned into a cross between a ninja and a ballet dancer. He vaulted into the air, spun in midleap, landed in front of the table, and snatched the remaining *Verminoids Special Edition* game.

"Nice job," the Greenblatt's employee said, offering Barrett a high five.

While Barrett did the chicken dance, I borrowed the employee's marker and grabbed the game out of his hands.

"Hey!"

"Relax," I said, flip-ping over the game box and laying the news-paper ad on top. Just as any detailed detec-tive should, I crossed

off everything we'd found. "CD—check! Book—check! Game—check! We're done!"

"Let's go check out," Barrett said. "I have an afternoon of gaming calling me!"

We made our way to the front of Greenblatt's and stood in line for what seemed like 45 minutes. The guy in front of us used a coupon, paid half by cash, half by credit card, and wanted a price match. The cash register apparently couldn't handle the math and spontaneously rebooted twice.

"They need to upgrade the software," the cashier said, yawning loudly.

As the guy left with a flat-screen TV that I'm pretty sure cost him $78, Barrett and I handed the cashier our purchases.

Beep! The CD rang up.

Beep! Dad's book rang up.

Beeeeeeeeeep! The video game didn't scan. The register displayed "ERROR."

The cashier tried again.

Beeeeeeeeeep! "ERROR."

"Sorry," the cashier said, "It must not be in the system. There's nothing I can do without a manager's approval, and all of them are too busy. Can you come back in a couple of days?"

"It should be in the system," I said to the cashier. "Your store advertised it for today." I pulled out the newspaper ad, flattening it carefully in my hand so she could see the advertised game.

She looked at the bar code symbol on the back of the video game and tried again.

Beeeeeeeeeeep! "ERROR."

"I think this is a clearance item," she said sleepily. "You'll have to come back later."

Barrett finally lost it. "It's not a clearance item!" he said. "It just came out today! It's the last one in the store!"

The cashier wrinkled her nose and leaned forward. "Sorry. I'm not much into video games. I can hold it for you."

Barrett looked as if he were going to explode.

"Be thankful," I whispered. "She's offering to hold it for you."

Then I said to the cashier, "That'll be fine." I started to pull out cash when I froze. "I think we should try ringing up the game again."

"I've already tried three times," the cashier said.

"Right," I said, "but there's something you need to know."

✷ ✷ ✷

Why didn't the video game ring up?

What are the clues?

Turn to the "Case Solved!" section on page 102 to find out.

ANT FARM AGONY

by Christopher P. N. Maselli

W HEN FACED WITH a mystery, a good detective knows you must always investigate the scene of the crime. Today, the scene of the crime was Matthew Parker's house. As we entered his kitchen, sunlight bathed the room, warming me to the bone. The white light flowed into the living room. A mirror in the living room reflected the light back, causing me to squint.

"*Whoa*—bright sun," Mrs. Parker said, welcoming us into the kitchen. She closed the blinds a bit. Then she waved at the dishes piled in the sink.

"Pardon the mess, Emily. We had a big cornmeal pancake breakfast for David earlier this morning—complete with blueberry muffins and orange juice, his favorite!"

"That's a pretty good Father's Day treat," I said.

Matthew nodded. "*And* we gave Dad a ticket to today's big baseball game. He's there now with one of his friends."

"You guys didn't want to go?"

Matthew's mom laughed. "I once went to a game with Matthew's father, and the next day my ears were still ringing from him yelling so much. He *really* gets into it."

I chuckled. "Understood. What's better on Father's Day than cornmeal pancakes and baseball?"

Matthew's eyebrows jumped. "You don't know the half of it. We have a lot more planned. When he gets back, we're going to play games and present him with a special honor."

On the kitchen table were several handmade cards from Matthew and his two sisters.

"Not those," Matthew said, noticing I was looking at the cards. "We got Dad a pet!"

"Oh no," I said.

Mrs. Parker sighed and left the room.

"What?" Matthew asked.

I put my hands on my hips. "You know what, Matthew Parker. Your family has a way of . . . okay, I'll just say it: Your pets seem to die in *mysterious* ways."

"They do not."

"What about that gerbil?"

"It—"

"And then the turtle?"

"C'mon! That's not fair! Even the vet said she couldn't explain that one."

"My point exactly," I said. "You know your family has no business getting another pet."

Matthew smiled wide. "That's where you're wrong!" He moved to the counter between the kitchen and the living room. Perched on one end was a plastic, rectangular box. He presented it with a grand gesture. "Ta-da!"

How I had missed it, I don't know. I was

obviously too pre-occupied with setting my sidekick straight.

"It's an ant farm!" Matthew exclaimed.

"You got your dad an ant farm—for Father's Day?"

"Do you know how hard ants are to kill? They only live, like, 60 days. Surely we can keep them alive *that* long. Even the cockatoo made it to 90. Besides, we wanted a pet that reminds us of Dad."

"Your dad is always interrupting people's picnics?"

"No! My dad is always *prepared.*"

I stared at him, blank faced.

"Like an ant prepares for winter. You know, like the Bible says. They are the *perfect* pets for the Parker family," Matthew continued. "It was my idea."

That didn't surprise me. Matthew has always been gifted at coming up with creative solutions.

That's part of what makes him such a valuable part of the Jones and Parker Detective Agency.

I peered into the plastic-cased ant farm, a labyrinth of sandy trails exposed to the world. My eyes scanned the tiny colony from one end to the other. The ants were surprisingly . . . still. I tapped the side of the farm.

Matthew grabbed my arm. "Careful! You could cause the trails to cave in and kill the ants."

"Um . . . I don't think that's gonna be a problem."

Matthew leaned forward and stared at the ant farm. He tapped the plastic case himself.

"Yep," I said. "They bought the—"

"Don't say it."

"—ant farm."

Matthew threw his head back dramatically. "How could this happen? We followed all the directions! Cooled them in the fridge so they wouldn't move too fast, then carefully placed them in the farm. We gave them a few drops of water and pancake crumbs from breakfast."

"At least they had a decent last supper."

"They're ants, Em. They'll eat dead flies. I don't think they noticed."

"Point taken. Did you expose them to direct sunlight?"

Matthew shook his head. "No, you can't do that or it could burn them up."

"Did you feed them after midnight?"

Matthew headed to the pantry. "I need some chocolate." He pulled the wrapping off a chocolate bar. "Em, we're supposed to be supersleuths! How come this happened? It must be some sort of fluke!"

"I don't think so," I said, confidently. "I think the answer is pretty clear."

❋ ❋ ❋

Do *you* know what happened to the ant farm?

What are the clues?

Turn to the "Case Solved!" section on page 103 to find out.

Case File #2011-09

THE MATH PROBLEM

by Christopher P. N. Maselli

MY SIDEKICK, MATTHEW PARKER, and I had just entered McAllister Park on our way to Whit's End to enjoy a couple of scoops of the best ice cream on the planet. Matthew would get chocolate; I'd get bubble gum.

The school day was over, and our backpacks were heavy. Solving a mystery was the last thing on our minds.

"Hey, Parker," Jay Smouse called out from one of the picnic tables. "Just the guy I'm looking for."

"Hey, Jay!" Matthew said, walking over to the table before I could stop him.

Jay Smouse. My brother's on-again, off-again rival.

Jay Smouse. Wannabe bully. Wannabe artist.

Jay Smouse. The kind of kid who delays your ability to satisfy a sugar craving.

Jay's math book was open, partly covered by a pile of shuffled papers.

"Whatcha doin'?" Jay asked.

"We're—" Matthew started to say.

"Help me with my math," Jay interrupted, pushing a piece of paper across the table.

Matthew shot me a glance.

"Why would I do that?" he said.

"Because if you don't, I'll—"

"I'll help you," Matthew said. "Besides, I like math."

As I thought about ice cream and bubble gum and the genius guy who put them together, Matthew stared at Jay's math paper. He twisted his lip, then handed the paper to me. "This is a bit tough."

I looked at the page. Jay had written the date and "Math pg. 49." Then he had scribbled down the problem in pencil. I read aloud, "Three-point-five twelfths plus two-point-five twelfths."

I stared at the problem. Matthew stared at the problem.

"Yeah, I remember study-ing this," I said.

"Can you explain it to me?" Jay asked.

I glanced around the park. Helping somebody who's annoyed me and my family so many times wasn't going to be easy. But I chose to be kind.

I nudged Matthew with my elbow. "Do you have a chocolate bar on you?"

Matthew slung his backpack off his shoulder, unzipped it, and produced a half-eaten chocolate bar. My sidekick is resourceful.

"Look! A squirrel!" Jay shouted, pointing to a tree.

I sat across from Jay and unraveled the foil. "Okay, forget the squirrel. Focus with me." I broke the bar into smaller squares. "Each of these is like a fraction of the whole," I said, spreading them out on a piece of Jay's notebook paper. "So if you take a decimal—"

"You lost me."

"I . . . what?"

"We've been in school like two weeks," Jay said. "We haven't studied decimals yet this year. We just started studying fractions. You know, like six-eighths and three-fourths."

Matthew grabbed a piece of chocolate and shoved it in his mouth. "I don't know if you should be taking math advice from her," he said to Jay.

"I'm *wholly* sure about that." I laughed at my bad joke, confident that if Jones and Parker ever closed, I could always moonlight as a comedian.

"Squirrel!" shouted Jay, pointing to the squirrel for a second time.

"Focus . . . ," I said under my breath.

I studied the handwritten problem again. This was rough stuff—not just decimals or

fractions—this problem had decimals *and* fractions mixed together. I mumbled the problem
aloud once more: "Three-point-five twelfths plus
two-point-five twelfths." Then I said to Jay, "Is the
answer in the back of the book?"

"You want to cheat?" Jay smiled at me. "Wish I'd
thought of that."

My face dropped. "I just want to work backward
from the answer."

Jay flipped forward a couple of dozen pages to
the answer key on page 170.

The answer to the problem was *four.* I shut my
eyes tight. How was that even possible? *Oh wait . . .
six-twelfths translates to . . .*

I let out a long breath and pushed the book
back to Jay. "You know what you need? Ice cream.
Come join us. I think you need a break so you can
think straight."

Jay frowned. "I *am* thinking straight. *You're* not
thinking straight." He grabbed his paper back. "But
I know ice cream would help—as long as you're
buying."

"Can I tell you something, Jay?" I love being
rhetorical. "Being kind would get you a lot further

with me. Which would be a good thing, because you need a detective to solve this problem."

"This isn't a mystery," Jay said.

"It *is* a mystery," I shot back. "The answer to this problem has *nothing* to do with math."

Jay looked at Matthew. "What is she talking about?"

Matthew nodded, a light coming on in his head. "She's saying you're focused on the wrong thing—and that's why this problem is so hard to solve."

✳ ✳ ✳

Do *you* know the solution to Jay's problem?

What are the clues?

Turn to the "Case Solved!" section on page 104 to find out.

Case File #2011-11

THE WAYWARD WHIRLYBIRD

by Christopher P. N. Maselli

SUNDAY IS SUPPOSED to be a day of worship and relaxation. Wake up, go to church, eat lunch with your family, read a book, watch a movie. My kind of day. But sometimes a mystery pops up, and you get a wrench thrown into your Sunday toolbox of fun.

I biked over to McAllister Park as soon as I got the call. My sidekick in crime solving, Matthew Parker, stood at the edge of a pond with a long tree branch in his hand, fishing for a plastic contraption floating on the water.

I skidded to a stop in the grass. "Hey, Matthew!"
Matthew threw me a glance. "Hey, Em, thanks for coming."

He sounded as if someone had just eaten his ice cream . . . and then stepped on the cone. Matthew reached down and pulled the contraption out of the water. It was a remote-controlled helicopter, shiny and wet.

I shivered. "It's cold out here, and I'm supposed to be relaxing at home."

"I can't relax," Matthew said. "Look at *this*."

He held up the helicopter and shook the drops of water off its propellers.

"What happened to it?"

Matthew let out a long sigh. "My invention failed. I designed it with Mr. Whittaker, but something went wrong."

He pointed to a small lip on the front of the helicopter. "It's a remote-controlled helicopter that delivers food to bird feeders high up in trees. You put the seed in here, fly the copter up, and drop the seed into the feeder."

I picked up the remote control. In addition to the up, down, and directional controls, there was a seed-release button.

"Can I ask a question? Why not just keep the bird feeder within arm's reach?"

Matthew wiped the helicopter blades on his shirt. "Because in a place like a park, you might not want the feeders where people can get to them. This allows you to keep the feeders out of sight and still feed the birds."

"That's actually pretty ingenious."

"I know! It would be perfect, if it hadn't just plunged into the water."

I grabbed the helicopter from Matthew and turned it over in my hands. "It's light."

"Mr. Whittaker suggested we build it light, with a plastic air bubble in the center. That's why it floated in the water. Thankfully, it was only 100 feet away, and there's a breeze. Otherwise, I'd be up to my elbows trying to fish it out."

"Too cold for that."

"You're telling me."

I paused for a moment and looked at the tree-tops. "Hey, maybe you flew it too high."

Matthew tilted his head at me. That was never a good sign. It meant I was about to get a lesson in science or mathematics.

"It won't go higher than 20 meters because that's the radius of the 2.4 gigahertz signal emitted by the remote control," he said. "Even if it *did* go higher, the signal would catch it again before it crashed. But in this case, that didn't happen. It's like it just lost the signal altogether."

I popped open the battery compartment. It was still dry inside.

Matthew shook his head. "There's nothing wrong with the battery. It typically lasts 20 minutes. I had it on for less than 5."

"What about the battery in the remote?"

"New."

Matthew took the helicopter and set it on the grass. He flipped a switch on the remote. The helicopter suddenly sprang to life. Apparently, it was waterproof. Matthew pushed a lever with his thumb, and the helicopter slowly lifted into the air.

He flew it up, then west, toward a large tree that

had lost all its leaves. The helicopter lifted higher and higher, until it hovered above the top branch. Matthew spun it around so it faced us. He pushed the seed-release lever, and it popped open a couple of times as if it were laughing at us. It made me giggle.

A moment later, it swept over our heads and then came to a peaceful rest at our feet. Matthew had controlled it masterfully.

"You've got nothing to worry about," I said, placing a hand on his shoulder. Sometimes sidekicks just need a little encouragement. "It works great."

"You think the dive into the water was just a fluke?"

"I didn't say that. But if you're flying this thing over people's heads and around birds, you need to make sure it works perfectly—otherwise you'll see some feathers flying . . . if you know what I mean."

Matthew grabbed the helicopter again and turned it around. He put his finger in the seed tray and fished out a drop of water. "Did I mention this thing flies on the 2.4 gigahertz spectrum?"

I stared at Matthew for a moment. "You did. That's pretty cool." It was a safe answer, even if I didn't totally understand what he was saying.

Matthew blinked twice and got a big smile on his face. "That's it! You're a genius."

"What's it?"

"I just figured out what was wrong with the helicopter. I know why it took a nose dive."

"You do? What happened?!"

✳ ✳ ✳

Do *you* know why Matthew's helicopter took a nose dive?

What are the clues?

Turn to the "Case Solved!" section on page 105 to find out.

Case File #2011-12

EUGENE'S NOT-SO-BRIGHT IDEA

by Christopher P. N. Maselli

IT'S UP TO a private investigator to figure out the key that correctly unlocks a mystery. Figuratively speaking, of course. Mysteries rarely have anything to do with actual keys. Sometimes they have to do with lights.

Thousands upon thousands of Christmas lights.

"Greetings and salutations, Jones and Parker Detective Agency," said Eugene Meltsner, all-around brilliant guy and technological genius.

"Hey, Eugene," I said.

Eugene was placing the finishing touches on his

gigantic Christmas light display at Whit's End. The front lawn was decorated with trees, a cross, reindeer, stars, presents, snowmen, wreaths, and about everything else seasonally appropriate.

"Was this your idea?" I asked. "I mean . . . making it *huge*?"

Eugene nodded proudly.

"I see you've used an infinite number of lights."

Eugene plugged one light set into another. Then he carefully stepped over a cord lying by a set of presents. "The lights are quite finite. There are exactly 12,801."

"Wow. And one," Matthew Parker echoed.

Eugene pointed to a yellow light on top of a tree. "A single star. It flickers."

I nodded. "Cool." Matthew stood with his hands on his hips. "So when do we get to see it lit up?"

"The sensor is set so the lights are on from dusk to dawn, so if the weather report is correct, it should be activated tomorrow night around 5:42 p.m.," Eugene said. "But since you're here, would you like a sneak peek?"

"Would we!" both of us cheered.

Eugene twisted his lips as he surveyed the magnificent display. A squirrel ran along the top of a nearby fence. Eugene looked at the sky, graying with the evening.

"Let's wait another 15 minutes for maximum effect."

Matthew and I sat on the chilled ground waiting for the time to pass. Once it did, Eugene circled around a large reindeer covered with lights.

"Prepare yourself!" he shouted as he plugged a single cord into the power box.

Fwump! We could actually hear the 12,801 tiny lights ignite, all at once.

Our eyes grew large as the technological wonder lit up around us like lights in a football stadium.

"Oooo," I said.

"Whoa," Matthew said.

"Excellent," Eugene said.

The squirrel covered its eyes.

The yellow star on top of the tree flickered.

Then the lights shut off. Completely.

Eugene's mouth dropped. "What?!" He leaned down to check the cord, but before he reached the box—*Fwump!*—the lights came back on.

"Oooo," I said.

"Whoa," Matthew said.

"Excellent," Eugene said.

The squirrel was frozen.

The yellow star flickered.

Then the lights shut off again.

Eugene bent down and quickly unplugged the cord. He crumpled to the ground. "Oh no, oh no, oh no. I must figure out the cause of this problem before everyone arrives tomorrow night."

Eugene plugged the display back in, stood up, and started checking all the electrical cords.

"You guys can go. I've got a long night ahead of me."

Matthew and I exchanged a glance.

"No," I said. "We're gonna stick this out with you as long as we can. If there's one thing your Christmas lights remind me of, it's that Jesus came to earth so we could walk in His light and help one another."

Eugene smiled. "I would be most appreciative. Junior detectives may be just what I need."

Together, the three of us checked the cords throughout the display, searching for any evidence. Of course, without the lights steadily on, it made it very difficult. A half hour later, we all stood staring at the snowmen, the trees, the reindeer, the presents, and the sometimes-flickering star.

The squirrel had clearly lost interest and was gnawing on a dark nut. I noticed both Eugene and Matthew eyeballing him.

"Hey," Matthew said, "sometimes on our Christmas tree there's a malfunctioning light in the chain that makes all the others blink. Could there be a bad light in your chain?"

"Not that I know of."

"Or maybe something's wrong with the breaker," I suggested.

Eugene thought about it, but then shook his head. He checked the plug again. "To borrow the colloquialism, there should be more than enough amperage for this circuit."

Matthew and I just stared at each other.

Suddenly, the squirrel popped up behind the power box. Eugene jumped from surprise and lost his balance. He fell back and knocked over the reindeer guarding the power box. *Snap! Crash!* Matthew and I ran to help him.

"Are you all right?"

"I'm fine, I'm fine."

Then Eugene froze.

"What?" Matthew said.

Eugene nodded. We looked behind us. The remainder of the Christmas light display shone brightly. Everything looked perfect.

"I see no rhyme nor reason to this," Eugene said.

"Maybe the lights on the reindeer drew too much extra power from the outlet," Matthew said.

I narrowed my eyes. "No, the key to this mystery isn't in the power. But I know what it is."

❊ ❊ ❊

Do *you* know what caused Eugene's Christmas lights to shut off?

What are the clues?

Turn to the "Case Solved!" section on page 106 to find out.

Case File #2012-06

PENNY'S NOT-SO-GREEN THUMB

by Christopher P. N. Maselli

As A DETECTIVE, you must learn to look under the surface of the facts. Don't just settle for the obvious.

I was explaining this to my sidekick in mystery solving, Matthew Parker, when Penny Wise nearly plowed over us.

"Oh, I'm so sorry!" Penny said as she ran backward, her big green eyes apologizing. "I'm running late. I have to water some plants and then go see Wooton at Whit's End before 4 o'clock."

"No problem," I laughed. "It's good to see you."

Matthew waved as Penny turned around, ran up the sidewalk, and entered a small, dark house.

"It's nearly 90 degrees, and she's still wearing a sweater and a hat," Matthew said. "I don't get it."

"She always wears a sweater and a hat," I said. "She says it's her trademark."

"I wonder if it's also her trademark to faint from the heat."

That's when we heard Penny scream. On instinct we rushed to the house and pushed the front door. It swung open, and we were hit with a blast of air-conditioning—a welcome relief from the hot outdoors. Penny was standing with a watering can in her hand, pointing to some potted flowers. The can looked as if it were about to fall from her shaking hand.

Matthew and I both followed Penny's gaze across the room. There, on the kitchen counter, sat a row of small plants.

"They're dying!" Penny exclaimed. "I was water-ing Mr. Henri's plants while he was on vacation in

Paris, but—oh no! Look what I've done. I've killed his plants!" Water from the can had puddled in the cups of flowers and was overflowing in the pot below.

Mr. Henri runs the art gallery where Penny works. He had moved to America from France a few years ago.

Matthew walked to the plants in question and flipped over the spotty, browning leaves in his fingers. "Yep, they're dying. I think they're violets."

"Violets!" Penny exclaimed. "As Mr. Henri would say, 'How *apropos*!' He told me that violets are supposed to symbolize modesty and humility. I told him that I could handle the plants as easily as he could eat a baguette. Now look at this! It should have been simple, right?"

Matthew shrugged. Penny put down the watering can and rubbed her forehead with her hands. She was clearly killing the plants, but my heart went out to her. After all, she was *trying* to do the right thing.

"You don't need to fret, Penny," I said. "We can solve this mystery. Matthew and I happen to be detectives."

"That's right," Penny said, looking distraught.

"And in this case, it's a mystery about the murder of innocent plants."

I took charge. "Matthew, why do you think they're violets?"

Matthew touched the plants again. "Partially because they have these soft, fuzzy leaves. But mostly because they're . . . violet."

Penny's eyebrows shot up. "You guys really *are* into deduction, aren't you?" She held up her right thumb. "I just don't have a green thumb. Look at it. It's like a little soldier that delivers death to all things leafy."

I grabbed Penny's thumb and pushed down her arm. "You're being too hard on yourself. We just need to figure out what happened. Did Mr. Henri leave you any instructions?"

Penny shook her head. "Just to water the plants for two weeks while he's away. I've been here every two to three days without fail."

I walked over to the blinds on the opposite side of the room. With a slight pull on the string, the sun pierced through, bouncing off a metal

decoration of the Eiffel Tower and bathing a
nearby fern with light.

Matthew's lip twisted. "Maybe the room wasn't
getting enough sunlight."

"I doubt that." I switched the blinds back to
their original position. Sunlight still basked the
room with a warm glow. "The room is relatively
bright. Certainly not dark enough to cause the
kind of damage that has appeared on those plants
within a couple of weeks."

"You watered *all* the plants?" Matthew asked.

"I treated them all the same," Penny assured
him. "I showered them with love and water."

Matthew pressed his fingers into the soil of one
of the violets. "The soil is pretty damp, and it's not
packed down too much. And the pot matches the
plant size."

I stared at Matthew. "How in the world would
you know that?"

He shrugged. "I learned it in earth science. I got
an A."

My sidekick never stops amazing me.

Penny threw up her hands in exasperation.
"Well, here's one girl who's gonna have to spend

a gazillion dollars on replacement violets at Gower's Flowers."

I looked at the browning plants once more, at the sunlit window, at the watering can, and then at Penny. "I don't think you should do that."

"Why not?"

"Because if you do, the same thing will happen again."

❖ ❖ ❖

Do *you* know why the plants are dying?

What are the clues?

Turn to the "Case Solved!" section on page 107 to find out.

BULLY BROUHAHA

by Christopher P. N. Maselli

CLUES AREN'T ALWAYS objects you find. Often clues reveal themselves in what you see and hear.

My sidekick, Matthew Parker, and I were taking the day off, because the carnival had come to Odyssey . . . and you don't need to be a detective to realize that means fun!

Our families had met just outside the ticket booth, where Matthew and I each bought five tickets to get started. We were on our way to the first ride when we (literally) ran into three well-known troublemakers—Jay Smouse, Valerie Swanson, and

Vance King. I accidentally bumped into Jay and dropped my tickets.

"Watch where you're going, Sherlock," Jay said.

I quickly picked up the tickets and stuffed them into my front pocket.

"Sorry," I said. "Let's go, Matthew."

I had only taken a few steps when my stomach dropped. I pulled out my tickets and counted. Only four. I counted again and felt my pockets. Nothing.

"What's wrong, Em?" Matthew asked.

"I've lost a ticket."

Matthew took the tickets from my hand. "You have a red one—that's for the Tilt-N-Whirl. The blue one's for the House of Mirrors. Yellow is for the bumper cars, and orange is for the Zipper."

"I'm missing green—the Ferris wheel."

Matthew and I scoured the area. Then we exchanged glances and turned our heads toward . . . the three bullies who were walking away. It wasn't often they all hung out together. They had a difficult time getting along with just about everyone, let alone one another. But the carnival has a way of building bridges.

Matthew and I ran over and stopped them in their tracks.

"Don't take another step!" I said.

Vance smirked. Valerie raised an eyebrow. Jay frowned.

"What's this?" Vance asked.

"Emily's missing a ticket for one of the rides," Matthew said.

"And this is our problem *why*?" Valerie sneered.

"Because," I said, "you guys saw me drop my tickets. I can't help but wonder if one of you snatched one."

Jay narrowed his eyes. "You calling us thieves?"

I put my hands in the air. "If I'm wrong, I owe you all a cotton candy. But let's face it. Matthew and I have solved dozens of cases these past few years, and each one of you has been involved in more than one."

Vance sighed. "Once a villain, always a villain."

Matthew shook his head. "We know that's not true. But you have to admit, history speaks for itself."

Vance grinned and turned to me. "All right. You're a detective, right?"

"Right."

Jay pointed to Matthew. "And you're her lackey?"

Matthew protested. "No, I'm her sidekick. I mean, partner."

"Well, if you're good at what you do, surely you know you're barking up the wrong tree," Valerie muttered.

Jay grabbed Valerie's arm. "Wait. I want free cotton candy. Let's let them see how wrong they are."

Valerie rolled her eyes.

Vance pulled his wallet out of his pocket. "Well, I've got plenty of money on me. I don't need to steal." He popped open the wallet, revealing a stack of purple tickets. "I'm playing games; that's all. No rides. So just purple tickets."

Valerie gave in and reached into her back pocket, pulling out a rainbow array of tickets. "Here are mine. As you can see, I bought only *one* of each color." She flicked the green ticket. "So this Ferris wheel ticket is obviously mine, not yours."

"And it couldn't have been me," Jay said. He pulled his tickets out of his pocket, one at a time.

"The black one's for the Tornado, the blue for House of Mirrors, the red for Tilt-N-Whirl, the pink for Wipeout, and purple for playing some games. I'm staying away from the Ferris wheel because I don't like heights."

I looked at Matthew. "What do you think?"

My sidekick shrugged. "It proves nothing."

"Aw, c'mon!" Jay shouted. "You're just trying to get outta buying us cotton candy!"

"Matthew's right," I said. "Jay, my ticket could still be in your pocket. Valerie could have mixed in my ticket with her own, and Vance could have turned in my ticket for more purple ones. Any one of you could have taken it."

Valerie put her hands on her hips. "You really *do* believe 'once a villain, always a villain,' don't you?"

"Just go to the ticket window and tell them you lost a ticket," Jay said. "Maybe they'll give you a new one."

"That's not necessary," I stated, "because I know what happened to my ticket."

"You do?!" Valerie's eyes grew wide. "This I gotta hear."

* * *

Do *you* know what happened to Emily's ticket?

What are the clues?

Turn to the "Case Solved!" section on page 108 to find out.

Case File #2012-10

THE TOOL TUSSLE

by Christopher P. N. Maselli

THE LONGER A mystery sits untouched, the harder it is to solve . . . so it's usually best to follow the trail of clues immediately.

My sidekick, Matthew Parker, and I heard a shout while returning from a hot day at the park. We ran to where we thought it had come from and found Red Hollard's tow truck propped up on a couple of jacks. His work boots stuck out from under the side.

"Red?"

"Stop, thief!" Red shouted from under the truck.

"Stop who?" Matthew said.

Red pushed himself out from under the truck. His hair was disheveled. His hands were dirty, and his work clothes were smudged with oil. In other words, Red looked like he always did.

"What were you screaming about?" I asked.

"Someone just stole my best screwdriver! I heard 'em run up, saw the shoes, the hand snatch, and then the escape. Whadayathinkathat?"

Matthew flipped open a notebook and started writing. "The thief took your best screwdriver?"

"Brushed aluminum with an ivory handle," Red said. "Had been sitting on the ground by the other tools while I worked. Got it from my uncle Quinton. He's a junk collector."

I peered down the street. "It doesn't sound like junk."

Red followed my gaze. "Wasn't to me. Probably isn't worth anything, but I want it back."

"And we can help you," I said. "What can you tell us about the shoes you saw?"

"Black sneakers with a navy-blue stripe," Red said.

"Mason South!" exclaimed a red-haired woman who'd obviously been listening to our conversation as she swept the steps of a nearby storefront.

I walked over and extended my hand. "Sorry? I'm Emily Jones."

"I'm Nellie," she said. "And I know Mason South wears black shoes with a navy stripe. He constantly steals little things from around this neighborhood. But he's clever, so you'll have a hard time proving it."

She gave us the location of his house.

"We'll find your screwdriver, Red," I said.

"Thanks. I just want Bessie back."

Matthew's eyebrow rose. "You named your screwdriver *Bessie*?"

Red raised his eyebrow. "That a problem?"

Matthew wrote something in his notebook.

We jogged all the way to Mason's house—a simple one-story brick house. We knocked, and a 20-something blond-haired man in need of a shave opened the door.

Matthew and I introduced ourselves. The young man told us he was Mason South. He wasn't wearing shoes, but I noticed a black pair with a navy stripe propped up on the wall just inside his entryway.

"Red Hollard's screwdriver was just taken from down the street," I said.

"And we're following up on some leads," Matthew added. "Are those your shoes?"

"Who cares if these *are* my shoes?" Mason exclaimed. "My brother Sam has a pair like these. I didn't take any stupid screwdriver."

Just then a sharp beep came from inside the house. Mason turned and shouted, "Sam, will you get that?"

When no one answered, Mason pushed open the door.

"I've got nothing to hide," he said. "I'm making some instant coffee. Come in."

Mason moved to the kitchen and opened the microwave oven. The door tilted slightly on its hinges. With an oven mitt, he pulled out a glass cup of steaming water. A plastic spoon, which had been resting on the lip, slid into the cup. Hot water sloshed onto the mitt.

"Looks like your microwave door needs to be

tightened," Matthew said. "You might need a screwdriver for that."

Mason removed the oven mitt and shook his head. "That's all you got? I can show you a hundred things in this house that need tightening. If I wanted a screwdriver, I'd have gotten one long before today."

"We're not leaving without Bessie," Matthew said.

"Who?" Mason huffed. He opened the coffee can and grabbed the spoon. "Yeouch!" He jerked his hand back, a stripe of red down his palm. He pressed it to his lips. "Now look at what you made me do! Sam!"

Finally, we heard a voice from the other room call, "I'm playing a video game!"

"Some kids want their screwdriver back!" Mason yelled.

The voice responded, "I don't know what you're talking about!"

Mason shrugged. "There you go. We don't have it. So you can leave now."

"We'll be happy to leave," I said, "once you turn over the screwdriver. You're lying to us, and I can prove it."

* * *

Do *you* know how Emily can prove Mason's guilt?
    What are the clues?
    Turn to the "Case Solved!" section on page 109 to find out.

Case File #2012-11

SCREAM FOR ICE CREAM

by Christopher P. N. Maselli

CLUES COME IN a variety of flavors. Sometimes they're right in front of your face. Other times they're hidden.

My sidekick, Matthew Parker, and I were discussing this topic when we were interrupted by the sound of screaming. When you're a detective, this means it's time to jump into action.

The scream of frustration came from an ice-cream truck parked a short distance away. The side of the boxy white truck read, "DOC's Ice Cream." Pictures of a dozen or so tasty-looking treats with their prices were scattered above the words "Edible for kids!" (Just in case you were wondering, Donald Oliver Cleese—known as Doc—always had a little trouble connecting with a younger audience.)

Matthew grabbed my arm. "Emily, are you sure we should check this out? Mr. Cleese competes against Mr. Whittaker's ice cream."

I laughed and kept walking. "C'mon. There's no competition. Whit's End is the best!"

We approached the truck and found Mr. Cleese sitting in the back. An old-fashioned wood-and-

metal ice-cream bucket sat between his feet.

"Mr. Cleese?" I called out softly.

The ice-cream vendor turned toward us, his hair messy and his eyebrow raised.

Surrounding him were milk and whipping-cream cartons, sugar bags, vanilla bottles, salt and pepper shakers, cups and spoons, and some mysterious small jars. Matthew didn't say a word.

I held out my hand. "We're with the Jones and

Parker Detective Agency. We heard you scream. Can we help?"

Mr. Cleese let out a long breath. "Not unless you can make homemade ice cream."

"*I* can make homemade ice cream," Matthew piped up.

I blinked. "You can?"

"Cooking is scientific," Matthew said, as if that explained it.

Mr. Cleese kicked the ice-cream maker at his feet. "I'm trying to make a new flavor of ice cream for the holidays."

My mouth started watering. "And the flavor is . . . ?"

"Turkey."

My mouth instantly dried up. "Excuse me?"

A smile broke onto Mr. Cleese's face. "It's the perfect holiday treat!" He grabbed one of the mysterious jars beside him, unscrewed the lid, and revealed about a pound of ground turkey.

Matthew pointed. "That is dis—"

"Delicious," I interrupted. "But wouldn't something like pumpkin pie be a better idea?"

"And possibly more *edible for kids*?" Matthew added.

I stared at Matthew. Sidekicks can be so unpredictable.

Mr. Cleese didn't lose a beat. "Clearly, you don't know kids very well."

Matthew and I exchanged glances.

Mr. Cleese continued. "For Christmas, I'm planning another flavor: mashed taters." He smiled. "There's a reason *I'm* the one with the ice-cream truck. You might be skeptical, but you'll find they don't taste half bad."

His words almost made me laugh, because I was thinking those flavors probably wouldn't be half *good*.

Matthew knelt, looking at the old-fashioned ice-cream maker. "So what's the problem?"

Mr. Cleese tapped his knuckle on the center canister. "I can't get the mixture to stiffen up. It just stays sloshy."

I took a closer look. "What are you doing differently than normal?"

"Making it myself," he said. "Usually I buy my ice cream from the store."

Matthew's head snapped up. "So this is your first attempt at homemade ice cream?"

Mr. Cleese tapped his knuckle on the side of his head. "All great ideas start somewhere."

I nodded. "So how do you make it?"

"With lots of love," he said.

"No," I said, "I mean, literally, *how* do you make it?"

Mr. Cleese raised an eyebrow. "With lots of love."

Matthew tried a different approach. "Can you show us the process?"

Mr. Cleese pulled out a new canister and mixed in milk, whipping cream, sugar, and a splash of vanilla. Then he added the ground turkey (it was cooked), along with sprinkles of pepper and salt.

He closed the canister and inserted it into the larger wooden bucket. He surrounded the canister with ice and started the machine that turned the ice cream.

"Are you done?" Matthew asked.

"No," Mr. Cleese said. He leaned down and gave the bucket a kiss.

It was awkward.

Matthew looked knowingly at the newbie ice-cream maker.

"I think I know why this isn't working," he said. "You left something out."

"What?" Mr. Cleese said, looking at everything surrounding him. "It's all in there."

Matthew shook his head. "No, it's not."

❉ ❉ ❉

Do *you* know what Mr. Cleese left out?

What would help stiffen up the ice cream?

Turn to the "Case Solved!" section on page 110 to find out.

Case File #2013-05

CASE OF THE MISSING DINNER DATE

by Bob Hoose

HAVE YOU EVER noticed how observant moms can be? They'd make great detectives. My sidekick, Matthew Parker, often talks about how his mom knows what he's up to before he even has time to actually do it. So when my mom told me we might have to change our plans for a celebratory "happy-birthday-hooray-Mom" dinner at a new Italian restaurant, I knew she'd observed something I probably hadn't.

"It's your dad," Mom said. "He's in his study,

going through some files for a friend from law school. If he doesn't come out soon, we're going to miss our dinner reservations."

"What?" I gasped. "He's the one who helped Barrett and me set everything up. Dad would never ruin your birthday."

"Oh, Emily, he won't be *ruining* anything." Mom smiled. "The church service this morning was wonderful. Besides, I don't need a fancy meal for my birthday to feel appreciated by you guys."

Mom's not the only observant one in the family. I noticed she was wearing her favorite dress and the earrings Barrett and I had given her after

church. No matter what she *said*, I knew this dinner meant a lot to her.

I walked over and opened the door to the study. "Dad, you've got to come with us. We've been planning this night for weeks."

My dad is a really good judge. He loves my mom (not to mention great Italian food), but he never rests until he's connected all the dots on a case. I could tell from the look on his face that he wouldn't be able to enjoy dinner unless this case was put to bed.

"I'm sorry, Emily," Dad said. "But I promised to sort through these files for a friend."

"Is there anything I can do to help?" I asked. "Maybe a little quick detective work?"

"I'm afraid this one's complicated." My dad sighed. "It has to do with a robbery in Connellsville and a group of teen thieves. I may have a lead on who's the real thief, but I want to make sure."

"Maybe another pair of eyes could help," I said. "And if I call Matthew, that would be *two* extra pairs."

"Make that three," Mom said, standing at the door.

With a smile, my dad gave in. In no time we were all in his study. Who knew where Barrett was. Probably playing video games.

"I can't stay too long," Matthew said while pulling a few books off the seat of Dad's overburdened chair. "I need to help my mom with chores in 10 minutes."

"So we definitely don't have time to check out the crime scene," I joked.

Dad gestured to the pile of papers on his desk. "That's what I've been doing this afternoon. These police reports are related to the case."

"Wow. You read *all* of these?" I asked.

"That's the life of a dedicated judge," Mom said.

For a second, I thought I saw Dad blush. "The police definitely caught the thief," Dad said. "They're just not totally sure which one he is."

Matthew looked confused.

"I can't go into all the details of the antique store break-in, but it's believed there was only one thief,"  Dad continued. "It's puzzling. These teen friends—let's call them John, Bruce, Dougie, Charlie, and Harry—are secretive types who refuse to give straight answers about anything. But the police conducted thorough interviews with them and several other witnesses. From studying all the transcripts, I've come up with a group of facts.

"First, the suspected thief and the group's

ringleader were overheard having a big argument, and someone heard the word *robbery* used.

"Second, the ringleader and Bruce play in a local video gaming tournament every Wednesday night. And John, one of the few in the group who owns a car, picks them up at 9 o'clock and drives them home.

"Third, Dougie is thought to really like the robber's sister, who was once going out with Charlie.

"Fourth, Dougie also works at the local bowling alley on weeknights and is thinking about taking a job at his brother's sports equipment store.

"Fifth, the ringleader is heavyset, and his mom works at the Connellsville supermarket. John, an only child, works there part-time as a stock boy.

"Sixth, Charlie is skinny and has been arrested for breaking and entering once before."

"Hmm," I murmured showing my notes to Matthew. "These *are* an odd bunch of facts."

"But I think we have enough to work with here," Matthew said.

"Yep." I smiled. "Not only can we figure out who is the ringleader and who is the thief, but we can also make reservations for Mom's birthday dinner."

"Sounds good to me," Mom said.

✾ ✾ ✾

Do *you* know who's the ringleader and who's the thief?

What are the clues?

Turn to the "Case Solved!" section on page 111 to find out.

Case File #2013-06

THE OPEN-AND-SHUT CASE

by Bob Hoose

"I SAW *YOU* leave the auditorium myself, Emily," Ms. Adelaide said, frowning in my direction. "Then I caught *him* in the hallway."

As I stood in front of the lockers between Vance King and Olivia Parker, I couldn't help but think how odd this felt. And not because Olivia was still dressed up in her emerald-green costume and rosy-cheeked makeup. I've helped solve many cases, but rarely have I been one of the prime suspects.

To give you the full picture, I ought to back up a little.

It was the last day of school. Tests were finished. Projects were turned in. All we had to do was clean out our lockers, watch a fun musical by the drama department, and then merrily begin our summer break. But about halfway through the performance, Ms. Adelaide had gone back to her classroom to complete some grading. That's when she discovered that the stacks of textbooks she had collected had disappeared.

She shouldn't have been totally surprised. Every year on the last day of school, somebody usually plays some silly prank. One year one of the bathrooms was filled with balloons. Another year all the whiteboard erasers went missing. But this was the first time I was a suspect, or Olivia Parker for that matter. Her brother (and my sidekick), Matthew Parker, stepped forward to vouch for us.

"I was sitting right next to Emily during the performance," Matthew declared. "She started coughing and left the auditorium for a drink of water. She was only gone for a minute or two. I can guarantee it wasn't enough time to take the books."

"How can you *guarantee* that?" Ms. Adelaide asked.

"I just walked the number of steps between the

auditorium and your classroom: exactly 179,"
Matthew said firmly. "She couldn't have run that
distance, hidden the books, and made it back in
the amount of time she was gone."

While Ms. Adelaide considered his argument,
I couldn't help smiling at my fact-focused friend.

"And my sister couldn't have done this, either,"
Matthew continued. "She was in the play, after
all."

"Yeah," the glitter-
covered Olivia chimed
in. "Why would you
think I took the
books?"

"Because I told her
you did it," Vance
said with a defiant
glint in his eye. "I
saw you do it, so
admit it."

Olivia gasped. "I didn't touch any books."

"You did too," Vance said.

"Did not," Olivia said.

"Did too—"

"Wait a minute, Vance," Ms. Adelaide

interrupted. "Why don't you tell me your side of the story."

"It's simple," he began. "I admit I wasn't in the auditorium watching the stupid musical. I was in an empty classroom. Jay was supposed to meet me to buy this old vinyl record that my dad gave me. Jay's into that junk. But he never showed up. Then I heard a locker slam. I stuck my head out of the door and spotted Olivia running from her locker. I know it's hers 'cause it's just a couple down from mine."

"But how do you know she had anything to do with the textbooks?" I asked.

"'Cause when she saw me," Vance went on, "she turned white as a sheet. She knew I'd caught her. She looked so guilty I knew it had to be something big. I went back in the classroom to wait, and when I came out, that's when you nabbed me, Ms. A."

"You weren't in every scene of the musical, Olivia," Ms. Adelaide pointed out. "You could have slipped away, so his story is at least plausible."

"I promise you I didn't do it," Olivia pleaded. "You've got to believe me."

"Hey, if you wanna find out for sure," Vance

smirked, "why not check her locker? It's right there."

We walked toward the locker, and Ms. Adelaide asked Olivia to open it.

"That's strange," Olivia blurted. "It shouldn't be locked. I already cleaned it out, and I left it open like we were told to."

When Olivia unlocked the locker and popped it open, it wasn't empty. Tons of textbooks nearly toppled out. Ms. Adelaide looked crest-fallen. Both Matthew and Olivia gaped with surprise.

"I have to admit," Ms. Adelaide said, "I'm disappointed."

"See?" Vance beamed. "What did I tell ya?"

"You did say Ms. Adelaide caught you right after you came out of the classroom, right, Vance?" I asked quickly. "You didn't go anywhere else?"

"No," Vance snorted. "I was waiting for Jay. Just like I told you."

"Well," I said, "I think we know who really hid the books, Ms. Adelaide. And it's *not* Olivia Parker."

❋ ❋ ❋

Who put the books in Olivia's locker?

What are the clues?

Turn to the "Case Solved!" section on page 112 to find out.

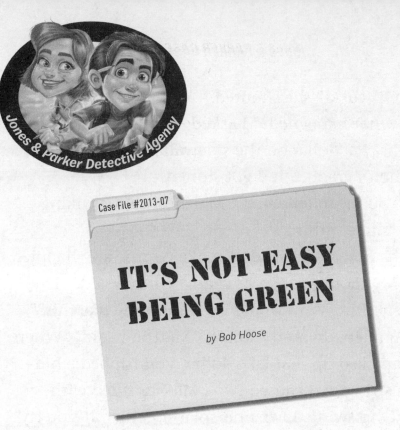

Case File #2013-07

IT'S NOT EASY BEING GREEN

by Bob Hoose

A REALLY, REALLY hot day can make you feel as if you're going to melt, but it doesn't keep mysteries from bubbling up. My mystery-loving sidekick, Matthew Parker, and I found our next case as we headed over to Whit's End to cool off.

I was dreaming of a fruity milk shake when I saw my friend Ginnie walking toward us. Suddenly, she stopped under a tree and picked a piece of paper off the sidewalk. Without warning, gobs of gooey green stuff splattered onto her head.

"Oh yuck!" she shouted.

"What happened?" I asked, running up to her.

"I saw a dollar on the sidewalk," Ginnie said. "When I grabbed it, I got slimed."

"You mean Jell-O-ed," Matthew said, walking up. "Lime, I think."

His observation didn't make Ginnie any happier.

"My mom's gonna be mad," Ginnie said. "This is a new shirt. Who would do something like this?"

"Somebody pretty smart," Matthew said. "When you picked up that fake dollar, you tripped a hidden string that caused two balloons filled with Jell-O to swing down and splat together. It's pretty ingenious."

"Whoever set this up is probably long gone," I said.

"I'm not so sure," Matthew said. "If he went to this much trouble, I'd guess the culprit would want to stick around and see if his trap worked as planned."

I glanced around. Jay Smouse sat across the street on a bench in front of Grocer Jenkin's store. The three of us made our way to where Jay sat, cool as a cucumber, sipping a soda. I had to admit his can of cola, all glistening wet with drips of running dew, looked deliciously cool and refreshing.

"Did you do this?" I asked. (The heat must've been getting to me. Normally, my questions are more clever.)

"Me? Nah," Jay said, almost smirking. "It is a real mess, though. Good thing she's got Parker and his sidekick to help her."

I could read right through Jay's little wisecrack. He wanted to make me mad and throw me off my game. Matthew grinned, and Ginnie continued to look sticky and miserable.

"That dried green spot on your shoe seems about the same color as the stuff that's all over Ginnie," I noted.

"Yeah," Matthew added. "And there's string hanging out of your pocket."

"It all looks pretty suspicious, if you ask me," I concluded.

"I didn't ask you," Jay replied, reaching into his pocket. "But since you're trying to pin this on me, here's everything in my pocket."

He had some change, a packet of candy fizzers, a rock, a worm, and a wad of partially chewed gum.

"What's the worm for?" Matthew asked.

"In case I want to go fishing later," Jay said. "I always keep lots of stuff in my pockets."

"I guess that explains the string," I said. "But what about your shoes?"

"These are my painting shoes," Jay said. "I was painting the fence at my house and got too hot. So I came over here for a cold drink. Take a closer look— my shoes have lots of different colored blobs on them."

"He's right," Matthew confirmed.

But Jay wasn't quite finished.

"Besides, I saw who set the trap. I've been sitting right here sipping this soda for a good 40 minutes.

I saw this tall kid run the string, plant the fake money, and put the balloons in the tree."

"You've been skulking around here for that long?" I asked.

"Hey, I'm a skulker," Jay replied. "It's what I do."

"At the very least, you could've warned Ginnie," I said.

"What, and spoil the fun?" Jay said. "And by the way, I'd swear that kid I saw setting this whole thing up was your brother, Barrett. So there."

"Do you think Jay's telling the truth?" Matthew asked.

I shook my head. "Stand back," I warned. "Jay's pants are about to catch on fire . . . and not because of the heat."

❋ ❋ ❋

How does Emily know Jay is lying?

What are the clues?

Turn to the "Case Solved!" section on page 113 to find out.

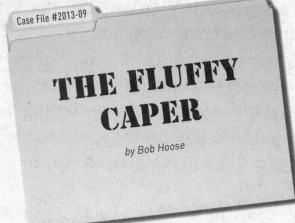

Case File #2013-09

THE FLUFFY CAPER

by Bob Hoose

RECENTLY A HAIRY case showed me the importance of barking up the right tree.

It all started on a sunny Saturday morning when my sidekick, Matthew Parker, and I were riding our bikes through Chatwick Hill. We like to pedal through this neighborhood from time to time because it's always fun to see what wealthy people put in their front yards. A waterfall here, a Japanese sand garden there, a detective with a magnifying glass over there. *What?!*

"All right, you two," the intrepid Harlow Doyle called out when he spotted us. "Where's the loot?"

"Where's the loot?" I replied as Matthew and I pulled to a stop.

"I asked you first," Harlow said. "Tricky word-play won't save you. Come with me."

With a wave of his hand, he turned and hurried off. We followed the detective around the corner of a big house and saw a rather large window with lots of broken glass covering the ground in front of it.

"Was there a burglary?" Matthew asked.

"Of course it's a bur-glary," Doyle replied. "As you well know, since you just returned to the scene of the crime. For shame, Junior Detective. I never thought you'd turn to a life of petty larceny."

"But—" Matthew started to say.

"Spill the beans!" Doyle interrupted. "What did you do with the valuables? Back at your hideout, eh?"

"We don't have a hideout," I said.

"Ah, *al fresco* felons!" Harlow said while pulling out a small notepad. "I'll make a note of that."

Just then an older woman stuck her head through the now glassless window. It was Mrs. Simmons, one of the Sunday-school teachers from church.

"Have you found Fluffy yet, Mr. Doyle?" she said before spotting us. "Oh, hello, Emily, Matthew. Did Harlow recruit your help, too?"

"Aha!" Mr. Doyle shouted as he wrote another note. "You know the perpetrators! That's the way it always happens in the movies. A textbook crime."

Mrs. Simmons assured Mr. Doyle that we weren't the culprits and invited us all to come inside to see the room where the theft had taken place.

"I still think we ought to keep these two in cuffs," Harlow grumbled as we walked into the house. "But since I lost my belt and need my handcuffs to hold up my pants, I'll just keep a steely eye on them."

The crime scene was a nice bedroom containing a desk, a few paintings on the wall, a thick mat in the corner, and what looked like a brass birdcage on its side near the window.

"Great twittering tweeters," Harlow said, gasping. He moved straight to the large metal cage. "The crooks have stolen your birds!"

"No, that's just an antique I keep in Fluffy's room," Mrs. Simmons said with a sigh. "I don't have any birds."

"I noticed a lot of valuable antiques in your house," I said to Mrs. Simmons. "Have you figured out everything that was stolen?"

"Oh, dear me, only one thing, as far as I can tell," the grayhaired lady replied. "My Fluffy. But he's the most precious thing I have."

Beating me to the punch, Matthew asked, "If you don't mind, what exactly is a 'Fluffy'?"

"My dog, of course. Didn't Detective Doyle tell you?" Mrs. Simmons put a hand to her heart. "This is his room. He's a beautiful Tibetan mastiff. A bit rambunctious, but my dearest dear."

"A Tibetan mastiff?" Matthew chimed in. "That

is a valuable dog. I read about a Chinese business-man who bought a purebred, longhaired mastiff for $1.5 million."

I stared at Matthew. "You read about dog sales?"

My sidekick shrugged. "Mom won't let us get a puppy."

"I must've surprised the thieves before they could take anything else," Mrs. Simmons continued. "When I heard the glass break early this morning, I rushed to this room, but Fluffy was gone."

"Plop, plop, fizz, fizz, I know who the culprit is," Mr. Doyle said, holding up a short lock of red hair that he found caught on the broken window. "And there's the *coup de grâce*," he crowed while pointing at a large boot print facing toward the window in the backyard. You could see where the boot had pushed some of the glass into the earth beneath it. "You kids are off the hook. We should be looking for a large, red-haired, one-legged man who's getting away with Fluffy as we speak."

I glanced at Matthew. He nodded in agreement, already reading my thoughts.

"Well, Mrs. Simmons," I said, "I think Mr. Doyle has indeed pinpointed the key clues to this mystery. But catching the culprit may take a bit more legwork."

* * *

What happened to Fluffy?

What are the clues?

Turn to the "Case Solved!" section on page 114 to find out.

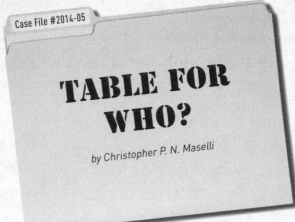

Case File #2014-05

TABLE FOR WHO?

by Christopher P. N. Maselli

SLEUTHING ISN'T JUST COOL, it's practical.
Situations often come up that call for someone to
restore a logical order to things.

This year on Mother's Day, Matthew Parker
and I decided to treat our mothers to a nice dinner in honor of all they do for us. Plus, we wanted
to thank them for their support of our detective
efforts.

We showed up at Chez Moi for a Sunday surprise. But much to *our* surprise, the restaurant was
full. Apparently, tons of other families had the

same idea. We stood behind someone who added his name to the lengthy waiting list. Then I asked Jenny, the hostess, to add "Jones" as well.

"It's a 45-minute wait," she said.

Matthew stared at me. "You should've made reservations, Em."

"Sorry," I said. "But it'll be worth the wait. This is Chez Moi. Authentic French cuisine. Mmm."

We went back to our families and sat down in the waiting area. We talked. We played a game on my mom's phone. But an hour later, our name still hadn't been called. Something was wrong.

Matthew groaned. "I'm starving. If we'd gone to Seven Seas, we'd be finished by now."

"Mother's Day is supposed to be classy," I replied. "There's nothing classy about fish sticks and coleslaw."

"Classy? Last time I checked, this place had snails on the menu!"

Some people just don't appreciate the finer things in life.

I went back to the hostess booth. Jenny looked nervous.

"Jones?" she said, scanning the list. "I'm so sorry, but I think we lost you."

"What do you mean?" I asked. "We've been here the whole time."

"One of the reservation sheets disappeared. Your name was probably on it."

My stomach sank. "We'll still be able to get in soon, right?"

"I'll do everything I can," Jenny said. "You're first on the list."

Just then a man approached, pulling a toddler boy by the hand.

"This is unacceptable!" the man shouted. "My family has been waiting forever."

"I'm so sorry," Jenny said. "Your name was?"

"Stephanopoulos. It's spelled how it sounds."

"Don't worry, sir," Jenny said. "You're first on the list."

Three other parties stepped up—Fogerty, Longfellow, and Rosas. All of our names had been lost. After talking to the manager, Jenny announced we would all receive free appetizers. But we still needed tables.

"You're first on the list," Jenny promised each family.

"We can't *all* go next," Matthew pointed out. "Some of us will have to wait again."

"I demand that you find me a table immediately!" Mr. Stephanopoulos yelled.

"I—I'm doing all I can," Jenny said.

"Maybe we can help." I smiled. "Matthew and I are detectives."

"It's true." Matthew pulled a notebook from his back pocket. "We'll figure out who got here first."

Jenny started to bite her nails. "It all happened so fast. Five groups showed up at about the same time, but I can't remember the order."

"Start with what you know," I suggested.

Jenny closed her eyes and tried to think. "The first person on the list was wearing red."

We looked around. I was wearing a red dress, while Mr. Rosas was wearing a red blazer. Mrs. Longfellow pointed out that she had a very attractive green purse.

"Anyone else remember anything?" I asked.

"You know, I don't think the party before *or* after us had any kids with them," Matthew said.

He interviewed the other parties. Mr. Fogerty

and his wife were celebrating their 40th anniversary. They had been looking forward to a quiet dinner for two. Mr. Stephanopoulos kept grumbling that he should have taken his family to Hal's Diner instead.

Mrs. Longfellow gently rocked her baby back to sleep. "I'm pretty sure I'm near the back of the line," she whispered.

"Not us," Mr. Stephanopoulos said. "We were in front of you for sure."

"That's not true." Mr. Rosas shook his head.

"I opened the door for Mrs. Longfellow before you arrived."

Mr. Stephanopoulos blushed. "Well, I'm not going last!"

My mom, always the peacemaker, buttoned her coat. "Maybe we should just go to a different restaurant. It's the thought that counts."

"Thanks, Mom," I said, "but we're not eating fish sticks today. Besides, we don't have very long to wait."

"That's right," Matthew said. "If you look at the clues, it's pretty obvious who should go first."

❊ ❊ ❊

Do *you* know the order in which the guests should be seated?

What are the clues?

Turn to the "Case Solved!" section on page 115 to find out.

CASE SOLVED!

Case File #2010-01,
"CASE OF THE SEALED SAFE"

"We had three clues," I said, holding up the checklist Dr. Swink had written. "The first clue was that the code has *three* numbers."

"That's right," Dr. Graham said. "But that doesn't tell us what the code is."

"Not directly," I said. "But Dr. Swink gave us another clue on the note he wrote to you."

"What do you mean?" she asked.

I held up the soggy note. "After writing down the combination for you, he wrote, *'My goodness. I can't believe it's been forty years!'* What do you think made him write that?"

"I know!" Matthew cried out. "The code must be the date he opened his office 40 years ago!"

I patted Matthew on the shoulder. "Exactly."

Dr. Graham frowned. "That's intriguing. But how do you know the date he started this practice?"

I held up the other paper. "Right here," I said, pointing to the fourth line. "'*Spend 5 minutes remembering what happened 40 years ago today.*' He purposely retired from this office 40 years to the day after he started. So try the number 12 for December, followed by 19 for the day he wrote this note, followed by two digits for the year 40 years ago."

"Forty-one," Matthew corrected. "It's January now, and he wrote the note in December." I've got to give Matthew credit—it's impressive when he keeps up.

Dr. Graham knelt down and swung the dial left, then right, then left again. *Click!* She pulled the lever, and the safe door groaned as it opened.

"You did it!" Dr. Graham said, pulling out some patient records. She smiled at us. "And to think I was going to call a locksmith. But now I know. I shouldn't have doubted you just because you're young."

"Now that you know what we can do, call us anytime," I said. "The Jones and Parker Detective Agency always cracks the case. And this time, we even cracked the safe!"

Case File #2010-06,
"MYSTERY OF THE VANISHING PAINT"

"Whit *did* see paint cans with green labels," I said. "And I can prove it."

"Please do," Mr. Watson said.

"Actually, what Whit saw were paint cans that *looked as if* they had green labels." I walked over to the large storefront window. "His eyes didn't deceive him, but the window did. See all this pollen?"

Matthew took the cue. "*Ah!* When the sunlight hit that pollen, it put a yellow light on everything inside—including the cans of paint with *blue* labels."

"But he saw *green* paint labels," Mr. Watson corrected us.

Mr. Whittaker smiled. "Of course! Because yellow light shining on blue paint would look green! And *that's* what I saw."

"Exactly!" I said.

Mr. Watson scratched his chin. "How did you two figure all of that out?"

Matthew held up his index finger. "Elementary, my dear Mr. Watson!"

Everyone groaned. I couldn't help but laugh at my sidekick.

"Nicely done," Mr. Whittaker said. "And maybe you've come up with your motto."

"What's that?" I asked.

"No mystery too hard, no *joke* too easy!"

Bible Evidence:

"For now we see through a glass, darkly."
—1 Corinthians 13:12, KJV

Case File #2010-11,
"THANKSGIVING *RUSH*"

"I know why you think the game's on clearance," I said.

I lifted the video game and showed the back to Barrett, setting the newspaper ad next to it. In all three places I had earlier placed three *X*s on the newspaper ad; the back of the video game had *X*s on *it*, too.

"I used a permanent marker to cross off the sale items," I said. "And because newspaper is thin, the marker soaked right through."

"So it messed up the box?" Barrett asked.

"Right," I said, "including the *bar code symbol* on the back. I realized that when the cashier said it must be on clearance—because a lot of stores cross out bar code symbols for any item on clearance so it won't ring up at full price. The scanner rejects it."

"Ah," the cashier said. "I should've noticed that; I'm just not used to waking up this early."

"Me too," I said. "So would you do us a huge favor and try *typing* the numbers under the bar code symbol instead?"

The cashier shrugged and gave it a shot—and the game rang up at the proper price.

Then the unpredictable happened: Barrett reached over and gave me a big hug.

Brothers. Even the lug-of-a-brother kind is something to be thankful for.

Case File #2011-06,
"ANT FARM AGONY"

Matthew popped the chocolate in his mouth. "I know what you're going to say. You're going to say the sun came through the kitchen window, reflected off the mirror in the living room, and cooked the critters. But that isn't it, because the sun just started coming through that window a little bit ago."

"No, that's not it," I said. "I'm afraid it *was* something found here at the scene of the crime, though: It was your mom's cooking."

"How's that?" Matthew asked, his eyes darting to the kitchen sink.

"Well," I said, "il wasn't so much her cooking as the *ingredients* she used. She said the pancakes were made out of cornmeal."

Matthew slapped his forehead. "Cornmeal! It's deadly to ants! And hours ago we fed it right to them."

"*Exactly*. People use cornmeal all the time to kill ants organically. The ants eat it okay, but water makes it expand in their stomachs, and they can't digest it."

"That's gross," Matthew said. "But another mystery solved."

"Can I make a suggestion?"

"No need," Matthew said. "I know what you're going to say: We don't have any business owning pets!"

I smiled. My sidekick was right on target.

Bible Evidence:

"Go to the ant. . . . Observe its ways and become wise. . . . It prepares its provisions in summer; it gathers its food during harvest."
—Proverbs 6:6, 8

103

Case File #2011-09,
"THE MATH PROBLEM"

"The answer," I said, "is to get to the root of your problem."

"I hate roots," Jay said, "and tubers. And any vegetable that's yanked out of the ground."

I smiled. "No, I mean you should ask yourself why this is so hard for you."

"I know what you're going to say," Jay said. "You're going to say I've been distracted by everything in the park. Like that squirrel. But I haven't." Jay narrowed his eyes. "The reason this is so hard, Sherlock, is because this is math, and I haven't learned it yet!"

"Calm down, my dear Watson," I said. "Because you're *right*. You haven't learned this yet. You're on the wrong page. I realized it when you looked up the answer. Not only was it not the correct answer to the problem, but you also

had to flip only about 20 pages to get to page 170. According to your own handwriting, you're supposed to be doing math on page *49*—which, if *my* math is correct, would be more than 120 pages away."

Jay's eyes dropped to the page in the book. "I'm on page *149*!" He flipped back to page 49 and slapped his forehead.

"Now how about you get a real brain freeze and join us for some ice cream," I said, truly trying to be kind.

But it was too late. Jay wasn't listening anymore. He was too busy pointing out the squirrel again.

Bible Evidence:

"Be kind and compassionate to one another."
—Ephesians 4:32

Case File #2011-11,
"THE WAYWARD WHIRLYBIRD"

"I realized the answer when I remembered something you said, Em," Matthew said.

"Glad to be of help," I said.

"You said maybe I flew the helicopter too high."

I narrowed my eyes. "But you said you didn't."

"That's true. But I also said the remote control's signal had a 20-meter radius. That means in every direction—not only up and down, but also side to side. The helicopter can't go more than 20 meters away from me, or I'll lose control."

My eyes widened. "And you specifically said it fell when it was a good 100 feet away. Since one meter is about three feet, that means you can't let it get—" I paused as I calculated.

"More than 60 feet away," Matthew said, finishing my thought. "I had it 100 feet away—too far. That's why it fell. It lost the signal."

"I knew you'd be able to figure it out," I said.

"Thanks, Em."

"Now let's get out of this cold. I'm supposed to be relaxing."

Matthew laughed. "Good idea. How about some hot chocolate?"

"Sounds great!" With that, we picked up our bicycles and rode to Matthew's house to enjoy the rest of our Sunday afternoon.

Bible Evidence:

"Anxiety in a man's heart weighs it down, but a good word cheers it up." —Proverbs 12:25

Case File #2011-12,
"EUGENE'S NOT-SO-BRIGHT IDEA"

"You're going to say the squirrel did it, aren't you?" Eugene said.

"Definitely not," I said. "That would be too easy. No, in this case, the problem was the reindeer."

"Right!" Matthew said. "It *did* take too much power—because it was so bright."

"Not exactly. The key wasn't the power it *took*, but the light it *gave*. It's all about the light."

"I'm not following," Matthew said.

Eugene tapped his foot. "I think I am!" He moved over to the power box. "This is a dusk-to-dawn power box, meaning it has a sensor to 'see' when it becomes dark or light."

"Exactly," I said. "When the sun goes down at dusk, the sensor turns on the lights, and when it's light at dawn, it turns them off. The problem was that the reindeer was sitting right in front of the box. So whenever the lights turned on—"

Matthew finished my thought. "The sensor thought it was morning. So it turned off the display. But then it was dark again, and the sensor calculated that it was night. So it turned the display on, then off. On, off, on, off."

"Indeed!" shouted Eugene. "Which explains why it works now that the reindeer has been removed from the equation. I must offer my thanks to you both. Now everyone will see my bright idea after all!"

Bible Evidence:

"If we walk in the light as He Himself is in the light, we have fellowship with one another."
—1 John 1:7

Case File #2012-06,
"PENNY'S NOT-SO-GREEN THUMB"

"What am I doing wrong?" Penny asked. "I *know* I gave them water and sunlight—just like every other plant."

"The key is to know what kind of plant you're dealing with," I said. "Because not all plants are the same. Some need more sunlight and water, some less."

Penny moved to the counter. "But aren't these violets?"

Matthew's eyes widened. "Yes! But we have to take the facts to another level. I read about these. They're *African violets*, and you're not supposed to pour water directly on the leaves . . . or they'll get spot damage. The leaves turn brown and ugly and look as if they're dying."

I stared at Matthew for a minute.

"Earth Science 101," he said, humbly.

"You probably got the leaves wet," I said, grabbing the watering can. "You said you treated all the plants the same, so you likely watered them from above."

"But you have to water African violets by pouring water in from the side," Matthew jumped in. "The water should hit the soil around them, not the leaves directly."

"That's it!" Penny exclaimed. "The murder mystery is solved. Even if I can't save these plants, I know what killed them. Now can you guys help me carry some violets back from Gower's Flowers?"

Bible Evidence:

"God resists the proud, but gives grace to the humble." —James 4:6

Case File #2012-09,
"BULLY BROUHAHA"

"Clues are sometimes what you hear," I said. "And the person who took my ticket is the one whose words gave her away."

Valerie twisted her lips. "I'm not following."

"I didn't think you would," I replied. "Because *you're* the one who stole my ticket."

"What?! Absurd!"

"Is it? When I questioned each of you, you were the one who specifically told me you didn't take my *green* Ferris wheel ticket because you had your own. And yet, we never told you *which* ticket was missing."

Matthew smiled. "Which means it *had* to be you. Only the culprit would know which ticket was taken."

Jay and Vance stared at Valerie. Jay said, "Way to go, Val! You just cost us our free cotton candy!"

Valerie peeled the green Ferris wheel ticket away from the rest of her own and slapped it into my hand. "Fine. You won fair and square."

I winked at Matthew. "All in a good day's work!"

Case File #2012-10,
"THE TOOL TUSSLE"

"I know you're guilty of something," I said, "because of the red stripe on your hand."

Mason winced. "You mean the burn I just gave myself? What's that got to do with anything?"

"You'd like us to *think* you just burned yourself . . . but we were warned that you were clever."

I walked to the cup and picked up the spoon. "Plastic doesn't conduct heat, so you didn't get that mark from this spoon. The missing screwdriver, on the other hand, was aluminum. Since it sat in the sun all day, it was hot enough to leave a mark when you grabbed it."

Matthew slapped his notebook shut. "The good news is Red said there are no hard feelings if you return it. But this is your one chance."

Mason stood and tapped his socked foot rapidly. Finally, he walked over to a drawer and pulled out Red's screwdriver.

"Here," he said. "I don't need it anyway. I just thought it looked cool."

"Thank you," I said with a smile.

Mason smiled for the first time.

"Red's a pretty good guy for forgiving me," he said. "Maybe I'll stop by to see if I can help him clean up his shop sometime."

Bible Evidence:

"Do not repay evil with evil or insult with insult, but with blessing, because to this you were called." —1 Peter 3:9, NIV

Case File #2012-11,
"SCREAM FOR ICE CREAM"

The ice-cream vendor looked one last time at the surrounding items. "I don't get it. I included everything."

"Maybe in the ice cream," Matthew said, "but not in the *ice.*"

I resisted the temptation to raise an eyebrow.

"The mixture isn't getting cold enough to become ice cream," Matthew said. "To make it colder, you have to add *salt* to the ice in the wooden bucket that surrounds the ice cream. Adding salt causes the ice to melt, stealing heat from the ingredients in the inner canister and dropping their temperature. It lowers the freezing point . . . so the ice cream firms up as you stir."

"Wow!" I said, "Cooking really *is* scientific!"

"It's something any wise ice-cream maker would know," Matthew whispered.

I smiled. Sidekicks really *are* unpredictable sometimes.

Mr. Cleese dumped a handful of salt into the ice surrounding the mixture and restarted the stirring mechanism. In a matter of time, the ice cream firmed up!

When it was finished, Mr. Cleese was so thankful to us for saving his dream that he gave us each a cone of turkey ice cream. You know, it wasn't half bad.

Bible Evidence:

"I, Wisdom, share a home with shrewdness and have knowledge and discretion."
—Proverbs 8:12

Case File #2013-05,
"CASE OF THE MISSING DINNER DATE"

"Okay, here's how we unraveled it," Matthew started out, as my dad and mom waited in anticipation. "Statement no. 2 tells us Bruce and John aren't the leader. Since the leader is stocky, he isn't Charlie. And since he plays in the tournaments on Wednesdays with Bruce, he can't be Dougie, who works nights."

"So," I jumped in, "the ringleader is Harry."

"This really is a sad case," Mom said. "These teens should be out building for their futures—not trying to cover for one another in a robbery. But the truth always comes out."

"Speaking of truth," Matthew said, "since Harry had an argument with the robber, that means he's crossed off the list of robbery suspects."

"Exactly," I said. "And the robber has a sister, so that leaves 'only child' John off the list."

"Uh-huh," Matthew continued. "And Charlie and Dougie are out, too, because one likes the robber's sister, while the other one used to."

"So that means the robber is Bruce," my mother said with a dash of deductive panache worthy of her mom-ness. "Crime solving is fun. Let's do some more."

"You guys all came to the same conclusion as I did," Dad grinned as he got up from behind his desk and tousled my hair. "Maybe Emily can give us a few more mysteries to chew on during dinner."

"That's fine," I said. "As long as you don't mind me talking with my mouth full. I'm starved!"

Case File #2013-06,
"THE OPEN-AND-SHUT CASE"

"You're crazy," Vance growled. "The proof is right there in her locker."

"Not really," I replied. "The proof of your guilt is in *your* story. First of all, you said you spotted Olivia running from her locker and she turned 'white as a sheet.' Well, that's impossible since she's wearing all this colorful makeup for the musical. I've never seen her look so rosy."

"Thanks." Olivia smiled.

"I was speaking, you know, allegorically," Vance said.

"Okay," I continued. "But you admitted that you knew where Olivia's locker was. So you could have easily put the books in her open locker to get her in trouble."

Vance gritted his teeth. "Yeah. Well, even if that's true, you can't pin this on me. What proof is there that I put the books in there?"

"None," I went on, "except for the fact you lied about what you were doing."

"Huh?" Vance said.

"You said you were waiting for Jay to sell him a record and he never showed up. So where's the album?"

Vance turned white.

"Since Ms. Adelaide grabbed you just as you came out of the classroom, and you don't have a record, your story has a crack in it," I summed up.

At that, Ms. Adelaide looked satisfied. Matthew and Olivia looked happy. And Vance, well, he looked like a record player that had just been unplugged.

Bible Evidence:

"Do not give false testimony against your neighbor." —Exodus 20:16

Case File #2013-07,
"IT'S NOT EASY BEING GREEN"

"What are you jabbering about, Emily?" Jay said, flustered. "I told you I had nothing to do with it."

"Ginnie," I said, ignoring him, "if we go to Jay's mom with his story, not only will you get an apology, you'll likely get a new shirt paid for with Jay's allowance money."

"No way," Jay said.

"Yes way," I said. "For starters, you said you saw the culprit set the string and place the 'fake' money."

"Yeah," Ginnie cried out. "How did you know it was fake from way over here? It looked real to me, and I was right next to it."

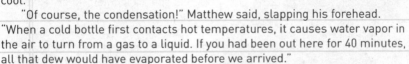

"Exactly," I went on. "And there's no way you've been sitting here for 40 minutes."

"I was," Jay blustered.

"Not possible," I said. "When we walked over, I saw your cola dripping with water and looking refreshingly cool."

"Of course, the condensation!" Matthew said, slapping his forehead. "When a cold bottle first contacts hot temperatures, it causes water vapor in the air to turn from a gas to a liquid. If you had been out here for 40 minutes, all that dew would have evaporated before we arrived."

"Well, I was really thirsty, and this is my second soda," Jay said.

"I'll go check that with Grocer Jenkin," I said.

"Don't bother," Jay said, throwing up his hands. "You caught me."

"And now you're the one who's all wet," Matthew summed up as Jay groaned.

Bible Evidence:

"These are the things you must do: Speak truth to one another; make true and sound decisions within your gates." —Zechariah 8:16

Case File #2013-09,
"THE FLUFFY CAPER"

"Mr. Doyle is definitely right," I said as I laid out the facts. "If somebody were going to steal a 100-pound dog, that person would have to be pretty big."

"But logic says the window breaker wasn't a man," Matthew said.

"Logic?" A flustered Harlow piped up. "How can you be logical at a time like this? There's a dog's livelihood at stake!"

"That's just it, Mr. Doyle," I went on. "I don't think Fluffy is in danger. In fact, he's the culprit."

"What do you mean?" Mrs. Simmons said.

"Well, first, the broken glass from the window was scattered on the grass

outside," I said. "If a criminal had broken in through the window, the glass would've shattered inward."

"But what about the boot print from the one-legged man?" Harlow said.

"That's probably *your* boot print, Mr. Doyle," Matthew said. "The boot pushed the glass shards into the lawn, so it happened after the incident."

"The best explanation is that Fluffy saw something outside last night, got excited, and accidentally knocked over the heavy birdcage," I said. "Then a bit of his fur caught on the broken glass when he jumped out the window."

"Tibetan mastiffs are bred as guard dogs, so they're alert at night and sleep more during the day," Matthew added.

"Great crunchy, wholesome goodness, you may be right," Harlow burst in. "Now let's just hope that pup hasn't already sold himself on the open market."

Bible Evidence:

"Stop judging according to outward appearances; rather judge according to righteous judgment."
—John 7:24

Case File #2014-05,
"TABLE FOR WHO?"

Matthew chewed on his pencil. "Well, we know the first person wore red, so that position belongs to Mr. Rosas or us."

"Right," I said. "And Mr. Stephanopoulos came in after Mrs. Longfellow. They were the last two."

Mr. Stephanopoulos scowled.

"But what about the rest of us?" Mr. Fogerty asked.

I reviewed Matthew's notes. "And since the groups *before* and *after* us didn't have kids, that puts Mr. Rosas and his red blazer first, then us, and then you. Mrs. Longfellow is fourth, and Mr. Stephanopoulos came in last."

"*¡Muy bueno!*" Matthew's mother cheered.

Everyone clapped . . . except Mr. Stephanopoulos.

"If you'll follow me, Mr. Rosas, your table is ready," Jenny said, smiling.

My mom gave me a big hug. "I couldn't be more proud of my detective daughter!"

Like I said, sleuthing is practical. And definitely classy.

Bible Evidence:

"Honor your father and mother . . . so that it may go well with you and that you may have a long life in the land." —Ephesians 6:2-3

Matthew Parker's Secret Codes

Matthew Parker's Mystery Decoder

See if you can fill in Matthew Parker's Mystery Decoder grid below and figure out this message. We filled in the letter *B* for you, and here are two hints:

Hint no. 1: 34-14-54-43-43-15-54 = ODYSSEY
Hint no. 2: There is room for only 25 letters in the grid, so *I* and *J* are combined. (You'll find out why later.)

Once you understand the code by figuring out how the numbers correspond to the grid, you can *write your own secret messages*!

42-15-43-35-15-13-44   54-34-45-42   35-11-42-15-33-44-43   &

31-15-11-14-15-42-43

_ _ _ _ _ _ _   _ _ _ _   _ _ _ _ _ _ _   &

_ _ _ _ _ _ _

	1	2	3	4	5
1		B			
2					
3					
4					
5					

See the answer on the next page.

Answer to Matthew Parker's Mystery Decoder

The first digit in a number indicates which row to use on the left. The second digit tells you which column to use on the top.

	1	2	3	4	5
1	A	B	C	D	E
2	F	G	H	I or J	K
3	L	M	N	O	P
4	Q	R	S	T	U
5	V	W	X	Y	Z

The answer to the code is *RESPECT YOUR PARENTS & LEADERS*.

More Fun!

This decoder was actually created about 200 years before Jesus' birth. The code maker was a Greek historian named Polybius. It's called the Polybius checkerboard. The Greek alphabet has only 24 letters, so in the original Greek code version, all the letters fit. To make 26 letters fit, followers randomly chose *I* and *J* to be in a single box.

Matthew Parker's Mother's Day Decoder

Can you find the pattern in the perplexing pairs below? Which letter in the pair is used and which letter is discarded? We've provided spaces for you to write the answer.

UH OV TN OR IR   YS DO UH BR

MI NO TE SH ED AR

__ __ __ __ __ __   __ __ __ __ __   __ __ __ __ __ __ __ __.

See the answer on the next page.

Answer to Matthew Parker's Mother's Day Decoder

This code is easy to write but difficult to break. Split the code into pairs of letters. For the first pair, ignore the first letter and only read the second. In the next pair, read the first letter and ignore the second letter. Switch back and forth, reading the second letter, then the first, then the second again until you've decoded every pair (as demonstrated in the bold, larger letters below). Got it?

u**H** **O**v t**N** **O**r **I**r **Y**s d**O** **U**h b**R**

Mi n**O** **T**e s**H** **E**d a**R**

More Fun!

Though cultures have celebrated mothers for centuries, it wasn't until 1908 that Anna Jarvis came up with the concept of Mother's Day after inviting friends to a memorial for her mother. For the next six years, she campaigned to get Mother's Day recognized. In 1914, it became an official US holiday. Tell your mom you appreciate her today.

Matthew Parker's Web Decoder

To bust this creepy code, you'll have to think like a spider! Each letter is located on a certain "strand" of the web. Some are close to the center. Others are farther away.

First, fill in the web below with the correct letters.

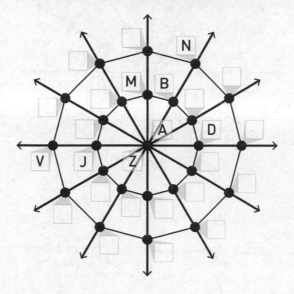

Then figure out which spoke is pictured below and look at the location of the spider (the dot) compared to the center of the web. Match that to the web decoder to get the letter. Got it? Now you can figure out what you're supposed to do when someone does you wrong.

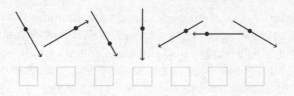

Answer to Matthew Parker's Web Decoder
Answer: FORGIVE

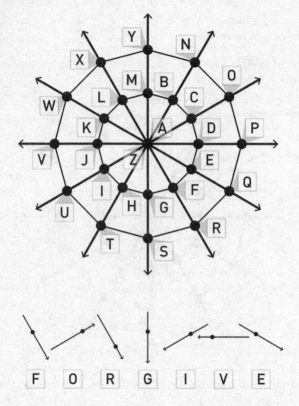

This puzzle was created by Christopher P. N. Maselli.

More Fun!
Certain materials like aluminum, copper, and diamonds conduct heat easily . . . but in 2011 scientists discovered another surprising source of heat conductivity: spider silk. The webs spiders weave actually conduct heat better than silicon and pure iron. This discovery could open the door to amazing new inventions, such as clothes with spider silk in them that take heat away from your body!